NL

R0201827904

01/2021

W9-AYO-603

PALM BEACH COUNTY
LIBRARY SYSTEM
3650 Summit Boulevard
West Palm Beach, FL 33406-4198

IGGY
IGUANODON

Bath Time & Bedtime

Time to Read® is an early reader program designed to guide children to literacy success regardless of age or grade level. The program's three levels correspond to stages of reading readiness, making book selection straightforward, and assuring that when it's time for a child to read, the right book is waiting.

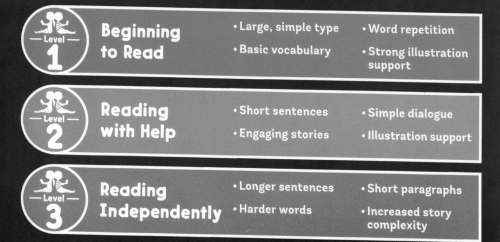

— Level 1 —
Beginning to Read
- Large, simple type
- Basic vocabulary
- Word repetition
- Strong illustration support

— Level 2 —
Reading with Help
- Short sentences
- Engaging stories
- Simple dialogue
- Illustration support

— Level 3 —
Reading Independently
- Longer sentences
- Harder words
- Short paragraphs
- Increased story complexity

For Nicolas and George Ryan—MM

For my Mother, the best
monster-checker-under-the-bed
a girl could have.—JF

Library of Congress Cataloging-in-Publication data
is on file with the publisher.
Text copyright © 2020 Maryann Macdonald
Illustrations copyright © 2020 Albert Whitman & Company
Illustrations by Jo Fernihough
First published in the United States of America in 2020
by Albert Whitman & Company
ISBN 978-0-8075-3641-4 (hardcover)
ISBN 978-0-8075-3644-5 (ebook)
All rights reserved. No part of this book may be reproduced
or transmitted in any form or by any means, electronic or mechanical,
including photocopying, recording, or by any information storage and
retrieval system, without permission in writing from the publisher.

TIME TO READ® is a registered trademark of Albert Whitman & Company.

Printed in China

10 9 8 7 6 5 4 3 2 1 HH 25 24 23 22 21 20

Design by Heather Barber

For more information about Albert Whitman & Company,
visit our website at www.albertwhitman.com.

IGGY
IGUANODON

Bath Time & Bedtime

Maryann Macdonald

illustrated by
Jo Fernihough

Albert Whitman & Company
Chicago, Illinois

Bath Time

Iggy Iguanodon was just like
all small dinosaurs.
He hated to take a bath.

"It's bath time, dear,"
Mama called.

"Not now," said Iggy.
"Maybe next week."

"Don't you want your scales
to look fresh and shiny?"
Iggy didn't care if his scales
looked fresh and shiny.

But all he said was,
"If I have to take a bath
then Stoog does too."

"Stoog took his bath yesterday," said Mama. "I'll take mine tomorrow," said Iggy.

"You'll take yours now,"
said Mama.
"Into that swamp!"

So Iggy plopped
into the steamy swamp.

The water was warm and sploshy.
He put his face underwater and blew bubbles.

Then he climbed up
onto the bank.

He slid back down
into the water.

Splash!

Splash!

SPLASH!

Iggy had a *lot* of splashing
to do.
So he had to stay in the
swamp for a long time.

Like all small dinosaurs,
he didn't like to get out of
his bath either.

"Bath time is over now,"
said Mama.
"Pleeeeeeease,"
Iggy begged.
"Just five more minutes!"

"No, dear,"
said Mama.
"You'll shrivel up."

So Iggy climbed out of the swamp and let Mama dry him off.

"Didn't you wash your neck and behind your ears?" she asked.

Wash? thought Iggy.

He knew there was *something* he had forgotten to do...

"Never mind," said Mama.
She gave Iggy a hug.
"We'll save that dirt for
next time."

Because like all mother dinosaurs, she loved her little reptile.

Bedtime

Iggy Iguanodon was ready
for bed.
He had shared a good dinner
with Grandpa.

He had splashed in the swamp.
Then his brother, Stoog,
had told him a bedtime story.
But now he couldn't go to sleep.

He kept thinking about
the awful creatures
in Stoog's story.

They were mean,
and they liked to fight.

"Don't worry about people,"
said Mama.
"They don't exist."

But all Iggy could think of were those scary beasts. What if one came into their cave?

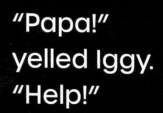

"Papa!"
yelled Iggy.
"Help!"

Papa stomped in.
"There *are* no people,
my boy," he said.

"It's just your imagination.
Now go to sleep."

But Iggy could not go to sleep.
He kept thinking about people.
They had smooth skin and
bony fingers and creepy hair
on their heads!

What was that shadow?
Was it a person?
Or just his imagination?
Iggy hid under the covers.

"Hah!" said Stoog.
"Scared you, didn't I?"
Iggy nodded.

"I used to be scared of people too," said Stoog, "but not anymore."
"Why not?" asked Iggy.

"Because Dreet told me that people would be afraid of us!"
"No!" said Iggy.
"Why?"

Stoog shrugged.
"Because we're different,"
he said.
"Different isn't always bad,"
said Iggy.

Stoog whispered,
"Want to know a secret?"
"Okay," said Iggy.
"Sometimes I like to be scared.
Do you?"
"Sometimes," said Iggy.

"Let's have a scaring contest!"
said Stoog.
"Let's pretend we're people!"
said Iggy.

Iggy and Stoog tried to
pretend quietly.
But it is hard to be scary
and quiet at the same time.

Sometimes there is a
crash or two.

Papa stomped in again.
"What's going on in here?"
he bellowed.

"Nothing, Papa," said Iggy.
"It's just your imagination."